Hello, Family Members,

Learning to read is one of the most important accomplishments of early childhood. **Hello Reader!** books are designed to help children become skilled readers who like to read. Beginning readers learn to read by remembering frequently used words like "the," "is," and "and"; by using phonics skills to decode new words; and by interpreting picture and text clues. These books provide both the stories children enjoy and the structure they need to read fluently and independently. Here are suggestions for helping your child *before*, *during*, and *after* reading:

Before
- Look at the cover and pictures and have your child predict what the story is about.
- Read the story to your child.
- Encourage your child to chime in with familiar words and phrases.
- Echo read with your child by reading a line first and having your child read it after you do.

During
- Have your child think about a word he or she does not recognize right away. Provide hints such as "Let's see if we know the sounds" and "Have we read other words like this one?"
- Encourage your child to use phonics skills to sound out new words.
- Provide the word for your child when more assistance is needed so that he or she does not struggle and the experience of reading with you is a positive one.
- Encourage your child to have fun by reading with a lot of expression . . . like an actor!

After
- Have your child keep lists of interesting and favorite words.
- Encourage your child to read the books over and over again. Have him or her read to brothers, sisters, grandparents, and even teddy bears. Repeated readings develop confidence in young readers.
- Talk about the stories. Ask and answer questions. Share ideas about the funniest and most interesting characters and events in the stories.

I do hope that you and your child enjoy this book.

       —Francie Alexander
        Chief Education Officer,
        Scholastic's Learning Ventures

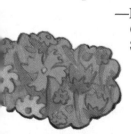

To my mother-in-law, Gloria

— L.B.

Go to scholastic.com for web site information on
Scholastic authors and illustrators.

ISBN 0-439-32095-X

Copyright © 2002 by Nancy Hall, Inc.
All rights reserved. Published by Scholastic Inc.
SCHOLASTIC, HELLO READER, CARTWHEEL BOOKS, and associated logos
are trademarks and/or registered trademarks of Scholastic Inc.

Library of Congress Cataloging-in-Publication Data

Hall, Kirsten.
    Green thumbs / by Kirsten Hall; illustrated by Lindy Burnett.
    p. cm. – (Hello reader! Level 3)
    Summary: Mrs. Wong offers a prize for the team with the healthiest plants in the
class spring project.
    ISBN 0-439-32095-X (pbk.)
    [1. Gardening—Fiction. 2. Schools—Fiction.]
    I. Burnett, Lindy, ill. II. Title. III. Hello reader! Level 3.
    PZ 7. H1457 Gr 2002
    [E] — dc21   2001049037

10 9 8 7 6 5 4 3 2 1   02   03   04   05   06
                        Printed in the U.S.A.
                      First printing, March 2002

Green Thumbs

by Kirsten Hall
Illustrated by Lindy Burnett

Hello Reader! — Level 3

SCHOLASTIC INC.

Cartwheel
·B·O·O·K·S·®

New York   Toronto   London   Auckland   Sydney
Mexico City   New Delhi   Hong Kong   Buenos Aires

Mrs. Wong's class had spring fever.
Outside, the sun was shining,
and the birds were singing.
Inside, Daniel and Pedro found it
hard to sit still.
Rika and Amy itched to go outside
and play.

"I'm glad everyone has so much energy," said Mrs. Wong. "You'll need it for our spring project."
She told the class they would be planting gardens.

The class would work together in teams.
She saved the best news for last:
The team with the healthiest plants would
win a prize!

"Want to be a team?" Rika asked her good friends Amy, Daniel, and Pedro. "Yes!" Amy said. "And let's divide our plot into four parts. That way we can each plant our own seeds."
The others agreed.

"I bet my plot will be the best," Pedro said. "I helped my grandmother in her garden once. Our plants grew this high! She said I had a green thumb."

Daniel didn't know if he had a green thumb.
He had never grown anything.
The next day after school, he went to the
library.

Daniel learned that plants start out as seeds.
In order to grow, seeds need sunlight, water,
and special plant food.

The next week, Mrs. Wong took the class
to a field behind the school.
"Class, this is where we'll plant our gardens,"
she said. "Each team will have its own plot."

"There's our plot!" Amy said. She pointed to
a section that had her name written on it. It
also had Rika's, Pedro's, and Daniel's names.

"Let's get moving!" Pedro said.
He drew lines in the dirt to divide
the plot into four parts.

Mrs. Wong put out large bags of seeds for the class.

Amy grabbed a fistful.

"I'll plant more seeds than anyone else," she thought. "That way, we'll have lots of plants to choose from. We'll be sure to win the prize!"

Amy poked holes in the ground with a stick.
Then she dropped a few seeds into each
hole.

Pedro read that plant food helps seeds grow. "I bet if I give my seeds lots of plant food, they'll grow faster than the other seeds," he thought. "Then our team will win the prize."

Pedro fed his seeds an extra dose of plant food.

Rika knew that seeds need water in order to grow.

"I'll make sure my seeds get plenty of water," Rika thought. "Then they'll grow big and tall, and we'll win the prize."

Rika poured a big bucket of water over the seeds.

Daniel remembered what the library
books had said about seeds.
Besides sunlight, seeds need water,
plant food, and room to grow.

Daniel followed the books' directions.
He planted some seeds in the ground,
putting space between each hole.
He gave them some plant food and water,
but not too much.
Then he waited for his seeds to grow.

The class visited their gardens every day.
On one visit, Amy saw her first seedlings
poke through the ground.

She was so excited, she planted more seeds.
She made dozens of holes with her stick
and dropped in the seeds.
Dig! Drop! Dig! Drop!

A few seedlings had sprouted in Pedro's plot, too.
But the seedlings didn't seem to be growing very fast.

Maybe his seedlings needed more plant food.

He added extra plant food to each seedling.

Sprinkle! Pat! Sprinkle! Pat!

Rika couldn't understand why
her plants weren't growing yet.
Other people's seedlings were sprouting.
Why weren't hers?

Maybe her seeds weren't getting enough
water.
She'd take care of that.
Splash! Splash! Splash!

Daniel's seeds sprouted right away.
He weeded out some of his seedlings
so the others would have room to grow.
He watered them every other day.
And he gave them plant food once a week.

Soon, Daniel's seedlings were bigger and greener than before.

His friends' seedlings didn't look as good. Amy's seedlings were tiny and too close together.

Pedro's seedlings were brown, not green.

Rika's seedlings were droopy.

Two weeks later, the four friends stood
in their garden.
"Your plants look terrific, Daniel," Amy said.
"And ours look terrible," Rika added.
"How did you do it?" Pedro asked.

"I read some great gardening books that showed me what to do," Daniel said. "And I didn't do too much."

"Then what's wrong with my plants?" Amy asked.

"The books said plants need room to grow," Daniel said. "You planted too many seeds, Amy. You need to take out some of your seedlings."

"Why are my plants brown?" Pedro asked.
"You gave your plants too much plant food," Daniel said. "If you leave them alone, they'll be green in no time."

"Why are my plants droopy?" Rika asked.

"You watered them too much," Daniel said.
"Water them less and they'll be fine."

Amy, Rika, and Pedro listened to Daniel.
Amy weeded out the seedlings that looked
the weakest.
Pedro stopped feeding his plants as much.
And Rika didn't water her plants as much.

A few weeks later, it was time for Mrs. Wong to inspect the gardens.
She carried a big bag of seeds to give to the winning team.
Mrs. Wong looked at all the gardens and admired the plants.

Finally she reached the last plot.
Amy, Rika, Daniel, and Pedro stood by their
garden, smiling.
They gave Mrs. Wong a large bouquet
of flowers from their garden.
"Why, these are beautiful!" Mrs. Wong said.
She took a deep sniff.

"I must say, these are the finest plants I've seen. How did you grow such pretty flowers?" She handed the team the bag of seeds.

"Daniel showed us what to do," Pedro said.
"And look! Now we all have green thumbs!"
He stuck out his thumb.
The four friends laughed.